British Library Cataloguing in Publication Data

A catalogue record for this book is available from
the British Library

ISBN 0-340-68090-3 (cased)

10 9 8 7 6 5 4 3

Published in French as LA GALERE D'OBELIX

Original edition © Les Editions Albert René, Goscinny-Uderzo, 1996
English translation: © Les Editions Albert René, Goscinny-Uderzo, 1996
Exclusive licensee: Hodder and Stoughton Ltd
Translators: Anthea Bell and Derek Hockridge
Hand-lettering: Ted Quelch
Inking: Frédéric Mébarki
Colouring: Thierry Mébarki
Co-ordination: Studio ETC

First published in Great Britain 1996 (cased)

Published by Hodder Children's Books
a division of Hodder Headline plc
338 Euston Road, London NW1 3BH.

Printed in Belgium by Proost International Book Production

GOSCINNY AND UDERZO
PRESENT
AN ASTERIX ADVENTURE

ASTERIX
AND OBELIX
ALL AT SEA

WRITTEN AND ILLUSTRATED BY UDERZO
TRANSLATED BY ANTHEA BELL AND DEREK HOCKRIDGE

HODDER AND STOUGHTON
LONDON   SYDNEY   AUCKLAND

To my grandson, Thomas,
and in homage to that great actor,
Kirk Douglas

GOSCINNYRIX

VDERZORIX

VIS COMICA

he power to make people laugh: from an epigram by Caesar on Terence, the Latin poet.

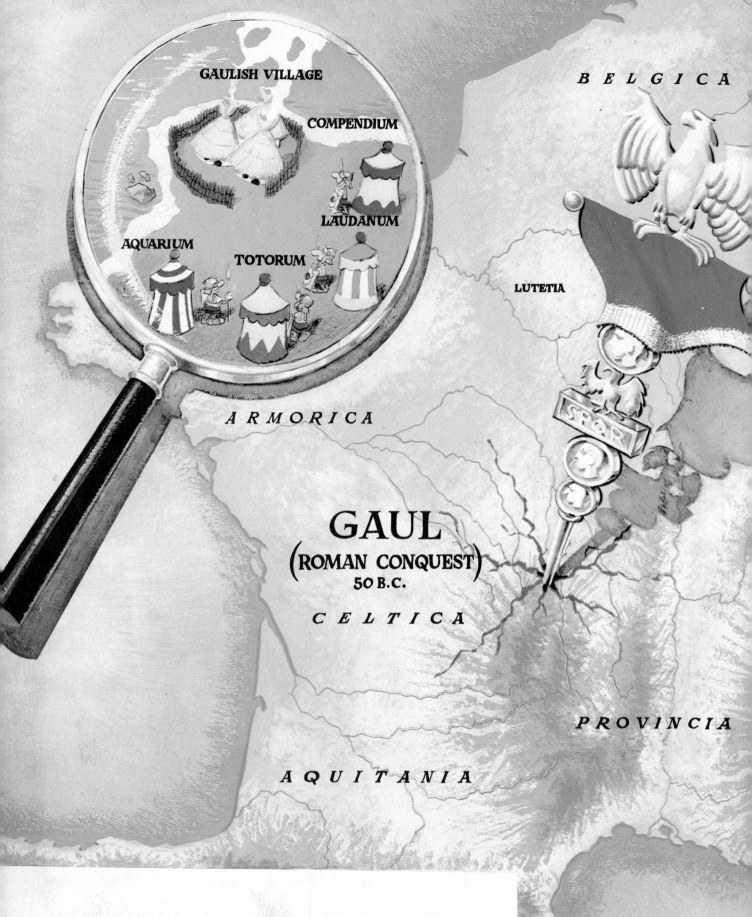

GAULISH VILLAGE

COMPENDIUM

LAUDANUM

AQUARIUM

TOTORUM

ARMORICA

GAUL
(ROMAN CONQUEST)
50 B.C.

CELTICA

AQUITANIA

BELGICA

LUTETIA

SPQR

PROVINCIA

The year is 50 BC. Gaul is entirely occupied by the Romans.
Well, not entirely… One small village of indomitable Gauls still
holds out against the invaders. And life is not easy for the
Roman legionaries who garrison the fortified camps of
Totorum, Aquarium, Laudanum and Compendium…

7

8

13

14

15

19

23

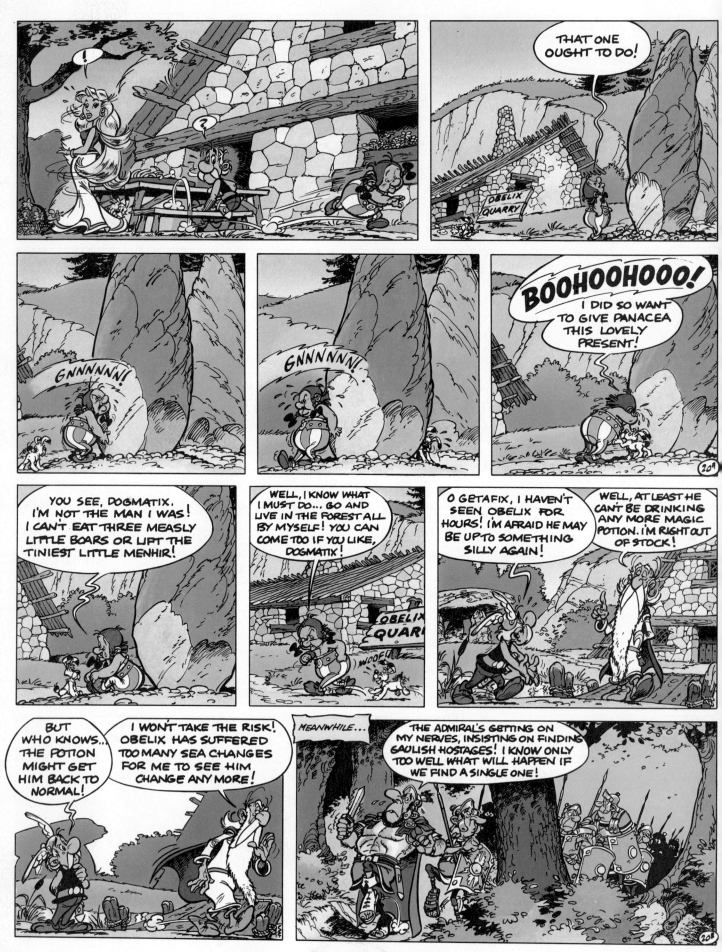

24

SURE ENOUGH, THE ADMIRAL'S SHIP, ALL SAILS SET, IS MAKING FOR OSTIA, THE PORT OF ROME, WITH A POOR LITTLE GAUL BELOW DECKS AND FEELING VERY LOW...

SO I GO BACK TO CHILDHOOD! SO I LOSE MY STRENGTH! THE ROMANS AREN'T AFRAID OF ME ANY MORE AND I'M THEIR PRISONER...

OH ASTERIX, PLEASE COME AND HELP ME OUT OF THIS!

WHAT ARE WE WAITING FOR? WE MUST CATCH UP WITH THE ROMAN SHIP AND RESCUE OBELIX!

MY CREW AND I ARE READY TO PURSUE THE ADMIRAL'S GALLEY, ASTERIX!

I'LL COME WITH YOU. I'VE JUST HAD AN IDEA WHICH MIGHT SOLVE POOR OBELIX'S PROBLEMS!

?!

HERE'S YOUR GOURD OF POTION, ASTERIX! I'VE FILLED THIS BARREL TOO, BECAUSE I WON'T BE ABLE TO BREW ANY MORE ON THE VOYAGE!

WE'LL KEEP IT AWAY FROM THE BARRELS OF DRINKING WATER, TO BE ON THE SAFE SIDE!

AND SOON AFTERWARDS...

WE'LL SOON OVERTAKE THE ADMIRAL'S SHIP, THANKS TO THE EFFECTS OF YOUR POTION, O DRUID!

YES, AND ONCE WE'VE RESCUED OBELIX I'LL TELL YOU MY IDEA, ASTERIX!

FLOP! FLOP! FLOP! FLOP! FLOP!

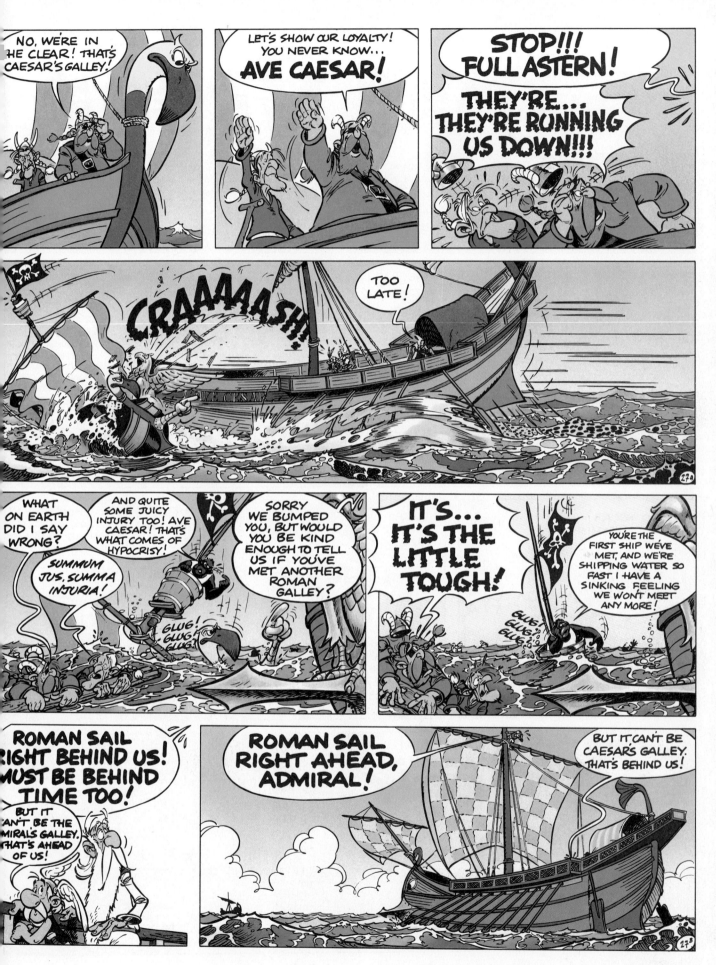

33

37

39

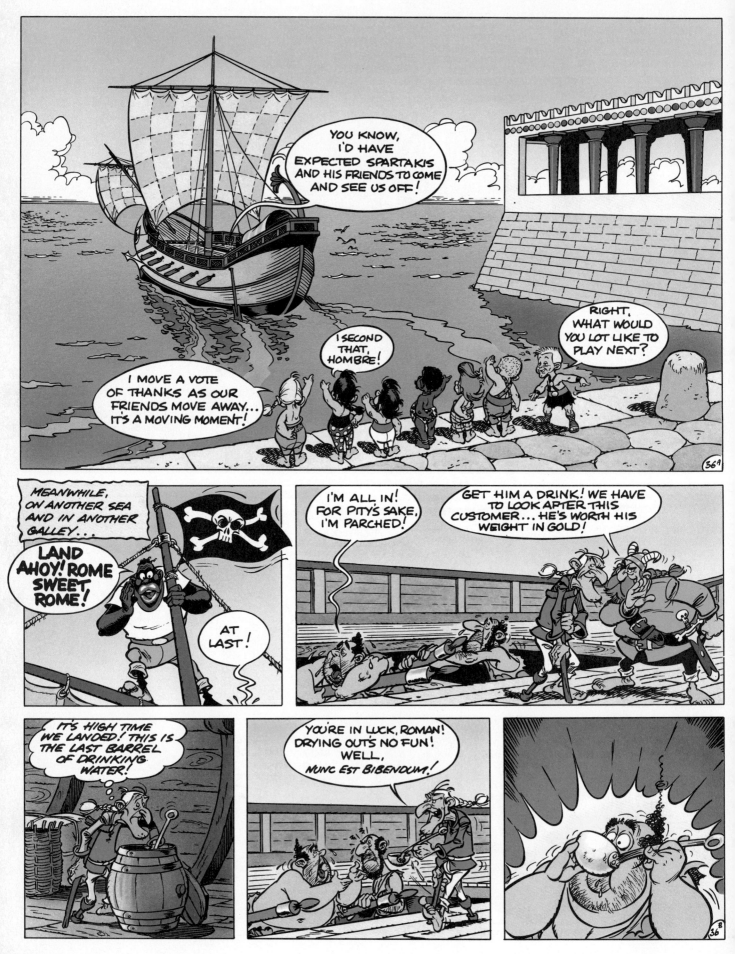

40

41